A CHILD'S CALIFORNIA

DAN HARDER

LAWRENCE MIGDALE

WestWinds Press™

Thanks to Ora (always, always, always),
to my two inquisitive sons, Joseph and Nathaniel,
and to my young weather friend, Gabe,
whose daily reading of the state's temperature helped to show me
just how wonderfully varied our state really is.
—D.H.

To my two terrific California kids, Daniel and Ari.
—L.M.

Text © 2000 by Dan Harder
Photographs © 2000 by Lawrence Migdale
Book compilation © 2000 by WestWinds Press™
An imprint of Graphic Arts Center Publishing Company
P.O. Box 10306, Portland, Oregon 97296-0306
503-226-2402; www.gacpc.com

Library of Congress Cataloging-in-Publication Data
CIP number: 00 038217
International Standard Book Number: 1-55868-520-0
Complete CIP information available upon request

Front cover: Thrill-seekers hold on tight at the California State Fair in Sacramento.

President/Publisher: Charles M. Hopkins
Editorial Staff: Douglas A. Pfeiffer, Timothy W. Frew,
Ellen Harkins Wheat, Tricia Brown, Jean Andrews, Alicia I. Paulson
Production Staff: Richard L. Owsiany, Susan Dupere
Editor: Linda Gunnarson
Designer: Constance Bollen, cb graphics

Printed on acid-free recycled paper in Singapore

OREGON

Crescent City
101

Redwood National Park

Eureka

Mendocino

CASCADE RANGE

Goose Lake

MOUNT SHASTA (Ele. 14,162')

5

Klamath River

Trinity River

Redding

Lassen Volcanic National Park

COAST RANGES

Great Central Valley

C A L I F O R N I A

395

395

Chico

5

99

80

Great Basin

Russian River

Cache Creek

Napa Valley

Sonoma

Santa Rosa

San Rafael

Golden Gate Bridge

San Francisco

Oakland Coliseum

Año Nuevo State Reserve

Berkeley
Oakland

Hayward

Silicon Valley

San Jose

Santa Cruz

Monterey

Salinas

SANTA LUCIA RANGE

COAST RANGES

80

99

Stanislaus River

Modesto

Merced River

101

San Joaquin River

Fresno

Kings River

MOUNT WHITNEY (Ele. 14,494')

Lake Tahoe

Sutter's Mill
Coloma
Sacramento

American River

SIERRA NEVADA

NEVADA

395

Yosemite National Park

99

5

California Aqueduct

Kern River

San Luis Obispo

101

Point Conception

Santa Barbara

Chumash Painted Caves State Historical Park

Malibu

WHITE MOUNTAIN (Ele. 14,246')

Bishop

Ancient Bristlecone Pine Forest

Owens River

Owens Lake

Death Valley

Los Angeles Aqueduct

395

Bakersfield

99

5

Los Angeles

5

15

Barstow

Mojave Desert

SAN GORGONIO MOUNTAIN (Ele. 11,502')

Joshua Tree National Park

Colorado River Aqueduct

15

Blythe

10

Colorado River

ARIZONA

Palm Springs

Salton Sea

PACIFIC OCEAN

N

0   25   50   75   100
MILES

✝ Missions along El Camino Real

◯ Special places you'll find in this book

Channel Islands

Santa Catalina Island

San Clemente Island

Legoland

15

5

San Diego
San Diego Harbor

8

MEXICO

Inset (Los Angeles area):

Burbank
Universal Studios

101

Pasadena

Hollywood Blvd

101

5

10

La Brea Tar Pits

Los Angeles

Pomona

10

Santa Monica

405

110

710

5

Torrance

Disneyland

Anaheim

◄ **Palm trees, sun, and rollerblade fun.**

▲ **Poppies burst into bloom after winter rains.**

---

magine a place where you can build a sandcastle on the beach, make a snowman in the mountains, then go down to the desert to see a breathtaking display of early spring wildflowers—all in the same morning. It's a very real place, and it's called California.

◄ **Monarch butterflies add color to a California spring.**

▲ **Snow makes a playground of the mountains in winter.**

From seaweed to cactus, black bears to monarch butterflies, dinosaur bones to microchips, California is filled with contrasts. Take, for example, a few of the highs and lows. The HIGHEST mountain in the continental United States—Mount Whitney at 14,494 feet—is only eighty-five miles from the lowest place in all of North America—Death Valley at 282 feet below sea level. No wonder on many a summer day, California boasts the hottest and coldest temperatures in the whole country.

▲ **The average annual rainfall in Death Valley—1.5 inches!**

▶ **A swimming pool is hard to resist on a hot summer day.**

California also can be very wet and very dry. Most of the state doesn't get much rain from April to October. That's why many native plants—like the yucca and the poppy—can live happy lives without sprinklers. In fact, one quarter of the state is covered with deserts, which occasionally get NO rainfall all year long. Now that's dry! And yet, these seas of sand are home to an amazing array of plant and animal life—some of which can only be found here.

◀ **A well-shaped wave is Nature's rollercoaster.**

▲ **Elephant seals "sing" at Año Nuevo State Reserve.**

But California isn't just one giant desert. Some places in Northern California get more than 120 inches of rain a year. And it's hard to get much wetter than the Pacific Ocean, which splashes against the western side of the state all the way from Mexico to Oregon. Grab a paddle, jump in a kayak, and keep your eyes open. In and around California's kelp beds, you'll find sea otters, countless fish, sea lions, migrating whales, and even the occasional great white shark.

▲ **Bristlecone pines often live more than 4,000 years.**

▶ **Hikers get the best views in the High Sierra.**

If you took your kayak to the northern coast, you could paddle past forests of the tallest trees in the world, the coast redwoods. And did you know that California's bristlecone pines are the oldest trees in the world? These gnarled and wind-twisted elders live in the high country of the White Mountains. And the world's thickest trees? The giant California sequoias in the mountains of the Sierra Nevada. A few of these trees are so humongous, you can drive a car right through them.

◄ **California coastal redwoods reign as the world's tallest trees.**

▲ **Wild birds are nursed back to health**

at the Lindsay Wildlife Museum in Walnut Creek.

Clearly California has many of "the mosts." Unfortunately, not all of them are good. Although it has "the most" kinds of plants and animals in America, it's competing with Hawaii for the state with "the most" number of endangered species. Still, many of California's endangered plants and animals are beginning to return to health—like the California condor (the largest bird in North America), the sea otter, and the mountain lion.

15

◄ ◄ **Albert Einstein is sculpted in Legos at Legoland in Carlsbad.**

▲ **You can play with optical illusions and other science wonders at**

The Exploratorium in San Francisco.

So what makes the California landscape so incredibly diverse? For one, California is BIG. It is the third-largest state in the Union. The dry southeast corner of the state is a long way (more than 1,000 miles) from the wet northwestern corner. California also has dozens of different mountain ranges—some tall and jagged, like the volcano and earthquake-formed Sierra Nevada—some weather-smoothed and rounded, like the Coastal Ranges.

Where there are mountains, there are valleys. Some of these are nestled high in the mountain landscape, like Yosemite Valley, where the other half of Half Dome was scraped off by a glacier many, many years ago. Other valleys in California are wide, open spaces set between completely different mountain ranges, like the Great Central Valley. Here, in this long and fertile stretch of green, you can pick a juicy orange from an orange tree, ride a tractor through fields of ripe tomatoes, or have a picnic under the shade of a majestic oak tree.

▼ **Ancient glaciers carved Yosemite and the face of Half Dome.**

▲ **Kids from many different ethnic backgrounds call California "home."**

▶ **Old traditions are given new life.**

alifornia's diverse geography is matched only by its diverse population. California has more of more kinds of people than almost anywhere in the world. And a whole lot of those people are kids—kids from Korea and kids from Texas, kids from Mexico and kids from Moscow. In fact, there are more kids living in California than in any other state in the United States.

And to help the people and products to move from one place to another quickly, Californians have built freeways—miles and miles and miles of them. As a result, California's cities have grown out, not up.

◀ **Friendship and face paint on the beach.**

▲ **A mother and child stroll past San Francisco's charms, both old and new.**

———————

In fact, in Southern California, San Diego and Los Angeles have spread so far that they've begun to blend into each other like two pancakes in a pan. So maybe they should call this new city Los Diego. Or is San Angeles better? Whatever they call it, this megalopolis is almost as big as the entire state of Connecticut. And in Northern California, San Francisco, other Bay Area cities, and Sacramento (the state capital) are beginning to ease into one another.

Because the cities are so big, there's lots to do in them—like watch a major league baseball game, stare into the eyes of a life-sized dinosaur at Universal Studios, join a dragon dance in a Chinese New Year's parade, play claves for *Cinco de Mayo*, visit an aircraft carrier in San Diego harbor, go to a hip-hop concert at the Oakland Coliseum, ride a bike across the Golden Gate Bridge, or step into the cement footprints of a movie star on Hollywood Boulevard.

◀ **In San Rafael, even the sidewalk is a place to create art.**

▼ **A colorful dragon welcomes Chinese New Year.**

▲ **Making masks for the Mexican festival _Dia de los Muertos_.**

▶ **Californian kids sometimes have odd angles on fun.**

But cities aren't the only places where kids are having fun. You can fish for trout in one of California's many national parks or skateboard in the warm winter sun of Palm Springs. You can look for seashells on the beach near Mendocino or ride hot-air balloons above the grapevines of the Napa Valley. Or you can hike into the mountains behind Santa Barbara, hoping to get a glimpse of a California condor and a peek into a cave painted by the Native Chumash people.

◀ **A proud Yurok Indian girl poses in Native dress.**

▲ **Kids at LeConte Elementary School in Berkeley learn how to grow vegetables.**

A *mazingly, the first European* to describe California never even saw it. Spanish author Garci Ordonez de Montalvo wrote a romantic story about a treasure island "very near to paradise" just to the north of Mexico that was ruled by the beautiful Queen Calafia.

When the explorer Juan Cabrillo sailed to the coast in 1542, he remembered the story and named this new land "California"—the land of Queen Calafia. And yet, long before any European imagined California, this land "very near to paradise" was home to as many as 300,000 Native Americans from some seventy-five tribal groups, including the Miwok, the Chumash, the Ohlone, and the Tongva.

▲ **Mission Beach in San Diego is a warm and sunny place to play.**

▶ **Smiles abound after a day in Disneyland.**

More than two hundred years after Juan Cabrillo claimed California for the King and Queen of Spain, the Spanish began to move in. They built twenty-one Catholic missions, mostly out of adobe bricks, along *El Camino Real*. Starting in San Diego and stretching to Sonoma, each mission was placed no more than a day's walk from the next. In 1822, Mexico took control of California, and even more people came—often to work on the *ranchos grandes*. California's famous gold rush of 1849 and statehood in 1850 brought many more settlers. While the Native population rapidly declined, the non-Native population exploded. From 1850 to 1860, the number of people living in California quadrupled.

When most of the gold was gone, California beckoned with other opportunities. The warm and sunny climate makes California an exceptional place for farming (more kinds of fruits and vegetables grow here than in any other state). The wonderful weather has also made California a great place to shoot movies. In the early 1900s, the first film studios started to produce "moving pictures" in Southern California. Since then, California studios have created most of America's movies—from *Snow White* to *Star Wars*. The fastest-growing

businesses in the state, though, are in computers and electronics. California has become the center of the "e-world." With Silicon Valley as the "dot-com" capital, California's kids are as likely to be surfing the Net as surfing the waves at Malibu.

Imagine a place "very near to paradise" with so many interesting things to see and do.

That place is California. ⚡

GLOSSARY

ADOBE — A brick often used by the Spanish made of sun-dried earth and straw. Most adobe walls were then plastered smooth and painted white.

CAVE PAINTINGS — The dream-like red, black, and white creatures painted hundreds of years ago by Chumash Indians in the mountains above Santa Barbara are the most elaborate cave paintings found in California.

CLAVES — The smooth, hardwood sticks that often are used as percussion instruments in Latin music.

DINOSAURS — The remnants of many of California's former inhabitants—dinosaurs, saber-tooth tigers, and ancient sea-creatures—can be found at many places around the state, like in the ancient tar at the La Brea Tar Pits in Los Angeles.

DOT-COM — The suffix added to the new world of e-business and communications. Most "dot-com" companies come from the state where the Internet was developed—California.

EARTHQUAKES — Shaking of the earth caused by one large part of the earth's crust (a tectonic plate) moving against another. The edge along which these plates grind is called a fault, and California has a lot of them.

ENDANGERED SPECIES — Plants and animals at risk of extinction.

EL CAMINO REAL — Spanish for "The Royal Road." The road, little more than a dirt path when first cleared in the 18th century, that connected most of the missions to one another in California and Mexico. (Look for the mission bell and staff that mark this ancient route along various California highways.)

GOLD RUSH — On January 18, 1848, John Marshall found gold near Sutter's Mill, now the town of Coloma, in the Sierra Foothills. In 1849, when the news spread, miners rushed to California to get rich.

MEGALOPOLIS — A heavily populated area centered around a city or several cities. Los Angeles, with its many satellite cities and suburbs, is definitely a megalopolis.

MISSION — In 1769, the first Spanish missionaries and a small garrison of soldiers came to Alta (Upper) California from Baja (Lower) California to establish churches and colonize the Native Americans.

NATIVE AMERICANS (MIWOK, CHUMASH, POMO, OHLONE, TONGVA, AND OTHERS) — Although many Native American cultures no longer exist, some still survive and can be seen in celebrations at any number of the state's powwows.

RANCHOS GRANDES — Spanish for "large ranches." Mexico, not Spain, controlled Alta California from 1821 to 1848. This was the time when the *ranchos grandes* flourished with their *vaqueros* (cowboys) and colorful fiestas.